MW00902493

OCT 2 2 2008

RECEIVED

NO LONGER PROPERTY OF
SEATTLE PUBLIC LIBRARY

Copyright © 2008 by Pat Schories
All rights reserved
Printed in China
First edition

CIP data is available

Front Street
An Imprint of Boyds Mills Press, Inc.
815 Church Street
Honesdale, Pennsylvania 18431

Jack
WANTS A Snack

Pat Schories

FRONT STREET
Asheville, North Carolina